Code of the Samurai

By Tracey West

Based on "SAMURAI JACK," as created by Genndy Tartakovsky

SCHOLASTIC INC.

New York   Toronto   London   Auckland   Sydney
Mexico City   New Delhi   Hong Kong   Buenos Aires

**Visit Scholastic.com for information about
our books and authors online!**

ISBN 0-439-45555-3

Designed by Carisa Swenson
Special thanks to Steve Hagel and Larry Morris

12 11 10 9 8 7 6 5 4 3 2 1   3 4 5 6 7 8/0
Printed in the U.S.A.
First printing, August 2003

WHO IS JACK?

Centuries ago, the evil demon Aku rose from the bowels of hate to take over the world. But the young emperor of Japan defeated Aku with a magic sword, burying his remains deep within the earth. The world was safe . . . but not for long.

Centuries later, sparks of sizzling sunlight revived Aku's remnants during a total eclipse of the sun. Aku returned to Japan to seek revenge on the emperor. The emperor's soldiers fought bravely, but they could not defeat the demon's strange powers. Aku captured

the emperor before he could reach his sword.

But one hope remained. The emperor's wife took the sword and her young son and left Japan. She hid the sword with a secret sect of monks, and sent her son around the world to be trained as a samurai warrior. When he became a man, he returned to Japan, claimed the sword, and challenged Aku.

Aku and the emperor's son fought a spectacular battle. But before the samurai could destroy the demon with one final blow from his sword, Aku conjured up a time portal that sent the brave warrior spiraling far into the future.

The emperor's son found himself in a future shaped by Aku, a dark world filled with machines, aliens, mutants, pollution, and despair. From the moment he arrived, he used his samurai skills to fend off danger. Some street kids, impressed with his moves, nicknamed him "Jack."

And Samurai Jack was born.

Now Samurai Jack has one mission: to find a way back through time and destroy Aku, thus preventing this horrible future from happening in the first place. But it's not going to be easy. Aku has named Jack Public Enemy #1, and Jack's every step is dogged by Aku's minions.

That's the story, all right. But it's not the **whole** story. We know that Jack is a samurai, but what does that mean exactly? Well, read on! This book will reveal the history of the samurai in Japan, the training of a samurai warrior, and, most important, the Code of the Samurai — a code of honor and behavior that shaped the way samurai warriors lived their lives.

And, of course, you'll get an inside look at Samurai Jack and what makes him tick. If you thought you knew everything there is to know about Jack, you might be in for a few surprises!

The Evil That Is
AKU!

The Deliverer of Darkness. The Shogun of Sorrow. Those are just some of the names used to describe Aku, the powerful demon who dominates Earth in the future.

Aku is the greatest evil the world has ever seen. He can absorb an onslaught of arrows and shoot them right back at his enemies. He can shape-shift into any form he wants, from a stinging scorpion to a sharp-clawed eagle. Beams of fire spurt from his eyes, turning anything they touch into ash. No force on Earth can destroy him – except for Samurai Jack's magic sword.

So how did this demon become so powerful? The answer lies in ages past, back when the universe first formed. Three shining gods burst into life – Odin, Rama, and Ra. But so did a formless blob of inky black evil. The gods fought the evil in an epic battle, bombarding it with their weapons. In the end, one piece of the evil spiraled through the

galaxies and landed
on Earth in the time of the
dinosaurs. The evil remained trapped in
the ground for centuries, destroying anyone and anything unlucky enough to stumble across it.
For years, the evil waited patiently, bubbling and
festering, for something to bring it to life. Finally, Jack's
father, the emperor of Japan, decided to try to destroy
the evil, which threatened the people of his village.
The emperor consulted with his monks, who created a
special elixir. The emperor dipped his arrow into the
elixir, shot the arrow into the bubbling evil . . . and
Aku was born!
The emperor had failed. The monks' elixir did not
destroy Aku. Instead, it freed the evil and gave it a new
form. Aku got more and more powerful as the years
passed. Now the only one who can stop Aku is Samurai
Jack. But will the brave warrior ever defeat the evil demon?
Not if Aku can help it!

What is a samurai? Basically, a samurai is a warrior, but there's a lot more to it than that. To really understand what a samurai is, we need to go back in time – to early Japan.

Japan is an island nation in Asia. The people who first lived in Japan survived by fishing, hunting, and farming. The only problem was, most of the island is covered with mountains and volcanoes, where farming is impossible. Because of that, people started to fight over the land. Years of warfare gave rise to a warrior class known as the samurai.

The samurai were skilled fighters, and they soon became the wealthiest people in the empire. The highest-ranking samurai was called a **shogun**. The shogun commanded the national army. Below the shogun were the **daimyo**, rich samurai who owned land. Each daimyo had an army of lesser-ranking samurai warriors sworn to fight for him.

Although the history of warriors in Japan goes back to 660 B.C., the official beginning of the samurai period was in A.D. 1192. That's when a shogun set up the

MURAI

first samurai government. In those early years, samurai prided themselves on their fighting skills. They not only fought against other samurai, but also to keep invaders out of Japan.

Besides being great warriors, the samurai also developed a code of conduct. A samurai lived his or her life by the code, which stressed loyalty, bravery, and honor.

By the year 1602, Japan entered a more peaceful time known as the **Tokugawa** period. Samurai spent less time fighting and more time studying things like literature and history.

By the end of the Tokugawa period, cities had become the places of power in Japan, not farms. The samurai lords could not afford to keep up their lands and repair their castles. Samurai warriors had nothing to fight for anymore. Over time, the samurai class became less important, until it disappeared in 1871.

Although the samurai have been gone for more than 100 years, tales of their legendary skills and bravery live on. Countless movies and books have been created that tell the story of the samurai. And then there's Samurai Jack, whose story is just beginning.

SAMUR

When a boy was born into a samurai family, his destiny was already chosen: he was going to become a warrior. Training began when a boy was very young. Boys began school at age seven. By age ten, they were going to school for twelve hours a day.

In school, young samurai learned regular school subjects like reading and writing. But they also learned how to fight. Boys learned two basic skills: to defend themselves, and to attack. They were taught sword fighting, archery, and horseback riding.

By the time a boy turned thirteen, he could wear the armor of a samurai and earned the title of warrior. In some periods, the front of a boy's head was shaved to show he had become a man.

Samurai Jack's life began just like any other young samurai's life. But then Aku returned, and Jack's life changed forever.

BACK TO THE PAST

While traveling in Aku's future, Jack stumbled upon the village of his childhood. After centuries of neglect, the village was a ruin of the beautiful place it had once been. But being back home sparked memories in Jack's mind. He remembered the young samurai girl who became his friend . . . an encounter with a lone samurai warrior who battled fiercely to save his young child . . . the advice of his father and mother . . . and the older bullies who teased him, until Jack figured out how to trick them. All of these experiences helped shape the man that Jack would become. Seeing the ruins of his village saddened Jack, but it strengthened his resolve to return to the past and undo Aku's evil.

When a girl was born into a samurai family, her destiny was also chosen for her. Most samurai women were expected to marry samurai warriors and be good wives and mothers. Like boys, girls were trained in their roles from a very young age.

Girls also went to school, but they did not learn the fierce fighting skills that boys did. Girls from wealthy samurai families learned things like reading, writing, and how to behave properly in society. Many samurai women became poets, writers, and scholars as a result of their education.

Some samurai women, however, were allowed to study the martial arts. They learned how to defend themselves and some even became warriors.

One famous Japanese **kabuki** play is about two women warriors, sisters named Miyagino and Shinobu. Their father was murdered by a samurai named Shinga. The girls learned how to fight in secret, and then challenged Shinga to a duel. They killed Shinga, restoring honor to their family. The play shows that samurai women could be just as skilled and brave as men.

Jack and the Woman Warrior

Jack once met a woman warrior in Aku's world. She helped Jack escape an attack from Aku's minions. Then she traveled with Jack across the desert in search of a legendary jewel with the power to send Jack back in time. But when they reached the jewel, the woman destroyed it and then turned on Jack. She wasn't a woman warrior at all — she was Aku, in disguise!

As we've learned, a samurai warrior's training began at birth. Even after a man earned the title of warrior, he never stopped training and learning.

Here are just some of the things a samurai studied during training:

- ◆ horseback riding
- ◆ martial arts
- ◆ archery
- ◆ sword fighting
- ◆ mental discipline
- ◆ battle strategy
- ◆ good manners
- ◆ reading and composing poetry

When Aku captured the emperor, it was not safe for Samurai Jack to stay in Japan. Instead, his mother sent him around the world to train with warriors and heroes from different cultures. Jack wore a special symbol around his neck that identified him as the emperor's son, someone to be trusted.

In his travels, Jack grew from a boy into a man. He learned the basic skills of a samurai warrior, but he learned some extra skills, too. All of this extra training helped Jack to become a well-rounded warrior – the only kind of warrior able to take on Aku.

Over the next few pages, you'll find out about the different kinds of training Jack undertook to become a warrior worthy of his father.

Every Samurai warrior was skilled in **ken-jutsu**, "the way of the sword." In this fast style of fighting, warriors learned how to use their swords to attack as soon as they were removed from their scabbards.

A samurai's sword was his most prized weapon. The craftsmen who made swords were known as **swordsmiths**. They took their jobs very seriously. A swordsmith studied for years to learn how to turn steel into a sharp blade. Before making a special sword, a swordsmith might first take a bath and say prayers. Some samurai swords were even said to have special powers.

When Jack was a very young boy, he had a wooden sword to practice with. When he became a man, Jack was given his father's magic sword – the only sword in the world with the power to destroy Aku. Jack never goes anywhere without his sword. The hopes of the world are resting on Jack – and his father's sword.

THE MAGIC SWORD

What is so special about Jack's sword? This one-of-a-kind weapon has a long and mysterious history.

Long, long ago, Jack's father helped to bring Aku to life by mistake. Aku set out to destroy the emperor, but the gods Odin, Rama, and Ra, Aku's old enemies, came to the emperor's aid. They forged a sword for him, but it was no ordinary weapon. To make it, they drew from the strength and power inside the emperor himself. The emperor later gave the sword to three monks, who blessed it with extra powers.

That special blessing, plus the fact that the sword comes from Jack's bloodline, is what makes it so powerful. But Jack's father reminded him of one important thing.

"The sword is only a tool, but what power is it compared to the hand that wields it?"

Jack's father was telling him that the real power to destroy Aku was not in the sword — it was in Jack. Without a man of honor to use the sword, it would have no power at all.

W hen Jack's mother escaped from Aku, she left young Jack on a ship with Japanese merchants. As the ship sailed across the Indian Ocean to its destination, the sailors on board taught Jack the art of navigation.

These days, scientists use computers to direct the course of ships, planes, and other crafts from one place to another. But in ancient times, sailors had to rely on other methods to steer their ships. One simple way involved staying close to shore and using landmarks, such as tall mountains, to plot a course.

But on long journeys on the open seas, sailors couldn't use landmarks. Instead, they developed a knowledge of the sun, the stars, and the weather. For example, the sailors knew that cold winds blew from the north and warm winds blew from the south. They also knew that the sun rises in the east and sets in the west, so they kept track of the sun's position to help them keep on course.

What did they do when the sun went down? They looked at the stars, of course. Early navigators studied the science of astronomy, which looks at the stars and planets in the universe. Ancient people recognized that some stars formed groups in the sky. Those groups are called **constellations**. They imagined that the constellations formed pictures of people, animals, and objects in the sky — like when you connect the dots in a coloring book. They gave these constellations names and stories. In the 20th century, scientists determined that there are 88 constellations in the sky, and they still use the stars to help with navigation today.

THE GREAT HUNTER

When Jack studied the stars, he probably noticed a constellation called Orion, the Great Hunter. Orion holds a club in one hand and the head of his catch in the other. Even though Jack was transported into the future, where everything has changed, the constellations have stayed the same. Who knows? Maybe Jack gets some strength from seeing the great hunter, a figure as skilled and powerful as he is, in the sky overhead.

JACK SHOOTS TO THE STARS

Jack not only got to study the stars with the Japanese merchants, but in Aku's future he got to travel to the stars, too! Jack met up with a group of scientists planning to escape Aku's world in a rocket ship. They let Jack ride with them on one condition — that he help them fight a robot blockade set up by Aku. Jack took off with the ship and, wearing a jet pack, left the space pod to fight the robots. He destroyed the robots, but did not get back to the ship in time to escape with the scientists.

The Japanese merchants sailed across the Indian Ocean, over the Arabian Sea, and left young Jack in the lands of the Arabs. Although the desert was hot and harsh, Jack received a warm welcome from a tribe of Bedouins. During his time with the Bedouin people, Jack learned the skills of horseback riding.

Jack couldn't have had better teachers. The Bedouins prized their horses, who helped them carry heavy loads across the desert and ride to victory in battle. Most important, the Bedouins treated their horses like good friends. On a cold night, a horse might be invited into a family tent to sleep!

The first lesson Jack learned from the Bedouins was to make friends with a horse before trying to ride it or train it. During his time with the tribe he became an expert rider. And even in Aku's mad future, Jack never forgets to treat horses — and all living creatures — with respect.

ROBO HORSE!

When Jack first landed in the future, a race of talking dogs asked for his help in escaping from Aku's grasp. The evil demon forced the dogs to mine for jewels day and night. When Jack agreed to help them, Aku sent a huge army of robot beetles to stop him. Jack didn't have a horse to help him, so he built a giant robot horse out of the mining equipment, then charged into battle. By the end of the fight, the metal horse was dust, but Jack was still standing — and the beetle army was destroyed.

THE MAJESTIC ARABIAN

The Bedouins raced Arabian horses, a species of horse known for its beauty and strength. Because the Bedouins have always taken such good care of them, Arabian horses still get along especially well with their human owners today.

If Jack had received his samurai training in Japan, he would have learned **Jo-Jutsu**, or stick fighting. But because it was not safe for him to return to Japan, the Bedouins took him west, to the south of Africa. In some of the tribes there, boys were taught stick fighting almost as soon as they could walk.

Until they turned fifteen, boys practiced the art of stick fighting with tree branches. It might sound easy, but it's a skill that takes a lot of coordination and quick reflexes. Boys were not allowed to stab each other with sticks, and a stick fighting match ended as soon as blood was spilled.

One reason boys learned stick fighting was to prepare them to become hunters and warriors when they became adults. But until that time came, stick fighting matches were a form of entertainment for the tribe. Sometimes, villages would challenge each other to stick

fighting matches, like the way schools in different towns play base-
ball and soccer games against each other today.

Jack probably had fun learning the art of African stick fighting, but when it comes time for serious fighting, it's one skill he's
glad he knows!

ANY STICK WILL DO

Jack once encountered a peaceful tribe of monkeys who
needed to defend themselves from a greedy tribe of baboons that
were stealing their food. Jack taught the monkeys how to stick fight
using the tall sticks of bamboo that grew in the jungle.

There's more to being a samurai than learning how to handle weapons. Jack learned this after he left Africa and traveled to Egypt to study with the scribes.

About 5,000 years ago, the Egyptians invented a system of writing called **hieroglyphics**. Instead of letters, like we have in the English language, hieroglyphs use pictures to represent sounds or groups of sounds.

Jack studied hieroglyphics with other boys at a school for scribes. Learning hieroglyphics was a great privilege. Only boys were allowed to learn how to read and write, and they were usually upper-class boys. Classes were strict, and teachers often exacted harsh punishment on students who didn't pay attention.

It was hard work, but boys who learned to read and write could go on to become priests or study medicine. Of course, Jack had a different destiny. But the gift of reading and writing serves him well wherever he goes.

AN EGYPTIAN PUZZLE

In the future, Jack's knowledge of hieroglyphics saved his life in a battle with Egyptian shadow warriors. Jack read hieroglyphs to solve riddles and call upon the ancient god Ra, who helped him defeat the fierce warriors. But even Ra did not have the power to send Jack home.

After learning hieroglyphics in Egypt, Jack's next stop was Greece, where he learned wrestling, the oldest sport in the world.

Today, wrestling is a spectacle involving costumes, fireworks, and heavy metal theme songs. But for the ancient Greeks, wrestling was about just one thing: a competition of strength and skill between two men. The object was the same back then as it is today – to get your opponent off of his feet and onto the wrestling mat. To do that, wrestlers use moves called **holds** to try to topple an opponent. Greek wrestlers used a style of wrestling called **loose style,** which basically meant that they could use any holds they wanted to, unless they were too dangerous.

Wrestling was a pretty popular sport among ancient Greeks. It was part of the first Olympics. Young men even went to special wrestling schools. Jack learned the sport of wrestling from some of the finest teachers in the world.

GO SUMO!

If Jack had received his training in Japan, he might have learned sumo wrestling. This is a style of wrestling known as **belt style**. A wrestler can use his opponent's belt to try to take the opponent down. Today, sumo wrestling is an extremely popular sport in Japan. Sumo wrestlers are enormous men who must try to push each other outside of a twelve-foot circle in order to win the match.

THE DOME OF DOOM

After being kidnapped and imprisoned by criminals, Jack was forced to battle in the Dome of Doom, a crazy competition with other men who had been captured. Jack had to fight off champion after champion in a wrestling-style arena while crowds of spectators cheered. By the time Jack was through, he had put the Dome of Doom out of business for good.

Every samurai was required to master the use of a bow and arrow. It takes years of practice to develop the steady hand and eagle eye needed to hit a bull's-eye without fail. For Jack's training, he traveled to England to learn from the best archer in history – the legendary Robin Hood.

You've probably heard of him – he's the guy who robbed from the rich and gave to the poor. No one is sure whether Robin Hood really existed (although Jack probably has an opinion about that). About 700 years ago, people began telling the story of the hero in ballads. According to legend, Robin Hood lived in the forest, dressed in green, and saved the poor people of the land from the rich, cruel landowners. It's easy to see why he was a good role model for Jack.

Robin Hood's weapon of choice was the bow and arrow. They were used in England – and almost every continent in the world – since prehistoric times. The

English used the bow and arrow for hunting, battle, and sporting contests. Thanks to Robin Hood's training, Jack's skill as an archer has helped him save the day many times.

THREE BLIND ARCHERS

Jack once met three archers whose skill rivaled his own – and they were blind! Jack had to find a way to get past the archers to reach a wishing well with the power to send him back in time. Jack blindfolded himself and relied on his training to outwit the archers. But when he reached the well, he found that it was cursed. Jack had to destroy the well, and thus lost another chance to get back to the past.

I n Arabia, Jack learned how to ride a horse. But sometimes a samurai must sail the seas. To learn the art of sailing, Jack traveled to Scandinavia to learn from some of the world's experts – from the **Vikings**.

Unlike Robin Hood, who robbed from the rich and gave to the poor, the Vikings didn't care who they robbed from. They sailed the seas, landing in towns and cities along the coast. Sometimes they traded goods with the people there, but they spent just as much time stealing and killing. In fact, the word "viking" means the same as the word "pirate."

Thankfully, Jack didn't pick up any bad habits from the Vikings. What he did learn was how to sail a ship on rough waters and in cruel weather. The Vikings sailed in longboats, sturdy ships made of overlapping wood planks. The longboat design was perfected so that the Vikings could travel long distances. Some reports claim that Vikings reached North America hundreds of years before Christopher Columbus made his famous voyage. Making such a long trip in an open longboat would have been extremely dangerous, but the tough Viking sailors never turned away from a challenge. When Jack left the Vikings, he was just as comfortable at sea as he was on land.

UNDER THE SEA

One of Jack's most memorable adventures took place under water. A race of sea monkeys lured Jack to their kingdom deep in the ocean with the promise of a time machine. But Jack didn't find a time machine there – he found a trap! Aku promised the sea monkeys he would return their kingdom above the waves if they helped him. But, of course, Aku didn't keep his promise. Jack escaped from the trap – and helped free the sea monkeys from Aku's grasp.

After training with the Vikings, Jack journeyed across the Baltic Sea to Russia, where he was taken in by people known as the **Cossacks**. The Cossacks first lived in the mountainous areas near the Black Sea and the Caspian Sea. They were known as some of the boldest and bravest warriors in the land.

Because they lived on the border of Russia, the Cossacks were often called upon to defend the country from invaders. Over the centuries, they became experts in handling many kinds of deadly weapons. Most Cossacks carried different kinds of curved swords, called **sabers** or **scimitars**. Some carried a weapon called a **pole-ax.** If a Cossack got knocked off his horse, he could use the pole-ax in hand-to-hand combat.

The Cossacks taught Jack which kinds of weapons were best to use in different situations. They also taught him how to throw a heavy ax with precision and skill — which is a lot harder to do than it looks.

Jack left the Cossacks, but he still had more to learn about hurling sharp objects at high speed. He crossed Russia into Asia, where he sought training in Mongolia. At one point in history, the Mongols set out to create a great empire by conquering Asia and parts of Russia. Led by Genghis Khan, the Mongol armies rode on horseback across the mountains, brandishing bows and arrows, and spears.

The Mongols taught Jack to use a spear like a warrior. The spear is one of the oldest weapons known to man. The first spears were long, sharpened sticks. Eventually the point of the stick was topped with a sharpened rock or piece of metal.

Like the Arabians, the Mongols were expert horsemen. It's likely they taught Jack the coordination needed to ride a speeding horse and brandish a weapon at the same time.

Growing up, Jack studied different forms of combat from warrior cultures around the world. But without discipline, all of this training would mean nothing. That's where the study of martial arts came in.

On the final part of his journey, Jack went to China to study with the **Shao-lin** monks. These legendary Buddhist monks hated violence, but they believed that the only way to stop violence was to learn how to defend against it. Over the centuries, the Shao-lin perfected a form of martial arts requiring concentration and self-discipline.

The monks started with ancient exercises called **t'ai chi ch'uan.** They developed movements that resembled animals: the bear, the bird, the deer, the monkey, the tiger, and, later, the snake.

When performed slowly, these exercises condition the body and relax the mind. But the movements can also be used to attack and defend against opponents in combat. **Kung fu** is a combat style that resembles the t'ai chi exercises of the Shao-lin monks. There are hundreds of styles of kung fu, and the martial art is still studied today.

Thanks to the Shao-lin monks, Jack learned not just kung fu, but the mental and physical skills he needs to survive in Aku's harsh world.

JUJITSU

If Jack had received his samurai training in Japan, he might also have learned a traditional Japanese martial arts style, such as **jujitsu**. Jujitsu is an unarmed martial art. Samurai practiced jujitsu to train their bodies to react quickly in sword combat.

THE CODE

Every samurai went through years of intense training to learn how to become a well-rounded warrior. But there was more to being a samurai than learning how to fight and survive. Each samurai lived by a code that helped guide him through life.

In the 1500s, the code was given the name **bushido**, which means "the way of the warrior." The bushido code evolved as the way of life in Japan changed over the centuries. But some basic ideas remained the same. A samurai vowed to become the best warrior he could be, an expert in combat who showed no fear toward the enemy. Qualities like kindness, honesty, and loyalty were also important parts of bushido.

Every decision Samurai Jack makes is shaped by this code. Jack knows that without the code, he would simply be a man who knows how to fight. A warrior who follows the code can be a hero; a warrior who does not follow the code is nothing more than a bully.

In these next pages you'll find out about the code that Samurai Jack lives by. If you know anything about Jack, then you know he's a man who takes his bushido seriously!

LOYALTY
A samurai must be loyal to his master

Long ago, a samurai's greatest duty was to his **daimyo**, or master. That meant that a samurai had to obey his master's every command and protect the life of his master, even if it meant losing his own life. Disloyalty to a master was considered shameful.

Samurai who did not have a master were called **ronin**. In the future, Samurai Jack is a ronin. He has no master that he must obey. Instead, Jack is loyal to his cause: to travel back in time and defeat Aku. Jack has risked his life to reach that goal time and time again, and he'll keep on doing it.

The Emperor

Back in the past, Jack's master was his father, the emperor of Japan. As an emperor, Jack's father cared for the safety of his people above all else. He taught Jack to care about the welfare of others.

When Jack was transported to the future, he had just freed his father, who had worked as a slave for Aku for years. When Jack finally does get back to the past, he hopes to see his father once more.

SACRIFICE

A samurai must be willing to give up everything

Many samurai enjoyed lives of privilege. They lived in beautiful homes. They spent hours listening to poetry or music. They went to see elaborate plays at the theater.

But at the core, every samurai had to be willing to give all of that up to serve his master. In a bigger sense, a samurai also had to be willing to sacrifice his own life if necessary.

For Samurai Jack, sacrifice is a part of every-day life. If he wanted to, he could find a quiet spot somewhere in Aku's world, or he could stay with some of the many friends he has made. He could choose to live out his days in peace.

But that's something Jack will never do. He will keep going until he destroys Aku, even if it means he will never find happiness. That's Jack's big sacrifice, but to him, it's defi-nitely worth it.

COURAGE
A samurai must have no fear

Samurai warriors were taught not to fear anything — even death. A warrior afraid of losing his own life might hesitate to save the lives of others.

In Aku's future, there is plenty to fear. Aku has spent centuries creating robots with the sole purpose of destroying life. After Aku ravaged planet Earth, he opened up portals to other galaxies so he could extend his power to other planets. As a result, all kinds of strange aliens populate Aku's future. Some are peaceful and kind, while others are fierce and willing to do Aku's bidding.

In his search for a way back home, Jack has had to battle robot beetles, expert alien hunters, a fire-breathing dragon, and even ultrarobots specially designed to defeat Jack in battle. But no matter what new horror Jack faced, he never backed down. He faced each enemy with fearless determination.

Jack and the Spartans

Once, Jack met an army of people just as fearless as he. The Spartans had defended their community from one of Aku's giant robots. The robot had an endless army of thousands of robot minions that it sent to destroy the Spartans. But the Spartans fought back for generation after generation.

When Jack met up with the Spartans, they decided to take a chance and get rid of the giant robot once and for all. Jack, the Spartan king, and fifty men faced off against an army of thousands of robots, but they did not back down. They bravely fought until the evil was destroyed forever.

KINDNESS

A samurai must help the helpless

Without kindness, a samurai warrior would be no better than one of Aku's minions. Every samurai was taught to care about the plight of others and help the helpless, no matter what the cost.

Kindness is one of Samurai Jack's key traits. Jack has met many people on his journey who needed help defending themselves against Aku's evil, and Jack has helped every one of them. Another person might say "tough luck" and keep walking, but not Jack. It's his duty as a samurai to help those in need.

Jack's greatest strength is also his greatest weakness. If he didn't stop to help those in need, he'd probably find a time portal a lot quicker. Jack has missed opportunities to get back home because he's been busy doing the right thing. But he wouldn't have it any other way.

The Woolies and the Critchellites

When you help others, you often receive help in return. That's what happened when Jack helped out the Woolies, a race of peaceful creatures that look like wooly mammoths. The Woolies had been enslaved by the Critchellites, a race of cruel monkeys who treated the intelligent Woolies like beasts of burden. The peaceful Woolies did not fight back until Jack showed up and helped them free themselves from the Critchellites. In return, the leader of the Woolies told Jack of a magic jewel with the power to send him back through time.

HONESTY

A samurai must be truthful

Never tell a lie. It sounds simple, doesn't it? But think about it. It's hard to be honest all the time. Like when your teacher asks you why your homework is late. Or when your grandmother asks you if you like the taste of her meat loaf. Normal people tell little white lies all the time. But for a samurai, being honest was a way of life.

In a bigger way, samurai also had to be true to themselves and to their nature. It would be very easy for Jack to turn to the dark side and join forces with Aku. No more running, no more fighting, no more hunger or cold. But Jack would never do it, because that's not who he is. It would be dishonest for Jack to join the side of evil. As long as Jack stays true to himself, there will always be hope.

The Scotsman's Wife

Of course, being honest can cause problems, too. In his travels, Jack befriended a Scotsman, a brave warrior on the side of good. The Scotsman asked Jack to help him rescue his wife from kidnappers. His wife turned out to be an extra-large woman with an equally large voice and personality. She took care of the kidnappers herself when they called her "fat." When poor Jack used the word "big" to describe her, she charged after him, too!

FRUGALITY

A samurai must live simply

To a samurai, living simply meant not having a lot of possessions to worry about. A samurai's most important possessions were his strong body and sharp mind.

Jack only owns a few things, and he can carry them all wherever he goes. He's got his white robe, his traditional wood sandals, and, of course, his sword. Sometimes he weaves a hat out of grass to keep his face shaded from the sun. But that's it. Think about it. Imagine if you had to carry your stuff with you wherever you went. You'd probably simplify things, too!

Jack's Sandals

Jack might only own a few things, but they're all pretty important. Once, Jack lost his wood sandals. He tried to fight a gang of bikers, but his bare feet couldn't withstand the heat and sharp surfaces of the rough city streets. The owner of a footwear store offered to give Jack any pair of shoes in the store. Jack tried everything from platform shoes to super pump-up sneakers, but he couldn't battle in any of them. Finally, he met a Japanese family who still kept to the old ways. They gave Jack a pair of sandals just like the ones he had lost. Back in business, Jack took care of the bikers.

DISCIPLINE
A samurai's training never ends

Jack's father once told him, "Always be alert to the presence of evil, my son, for it is sometimes right behind you."

A samurai warrior is always alert, always ready to face danger. To do this takes great mental and physical discipline. Even after a young samurai became a warrior, he never stopped training his body and mind. He continued to practice martial arts to keep his body strong. To keep his mind sharp and clear, he meditated or composed poetry.

In the future, Jack continues to train and learn new things. Without discipline, Jack would have fallen prey to Aku's minions long ago.

Jack Learns to Jump High

Jack learned a great new skill when he met up with a tribe of intelligent monkeys. They all had the amazing ability to "jump high." Each one could spring off of its feet and travel straight up in the air for hundreds of feet.

Jack taught the monkeys to defend themselves from a tribe of baboons. In return, they taught Jack how to jump high. It took hours of training. Jack ran up hills with boulders strapped to his feet and back. But when the boulders finally came off, Jack could jump just as high as his new friends.

MIND AND SPIRIT

A samurai must be strong in all areas

When you think of a warrior, you probably think of a super-skilled fighter. But samurai warriors made sure they were strong in mind and spirit as well as in body.

A samurai who followed Zen Buddhism might practice meditation. That's the practice of sitting quietly and clearing your mind of thoughts. Practicing meditation could help a warrior keep a calm spirit during tough times.

To strengthen their minds, samurai learned to read and write. They studied poetry and learned to compose their own poems. They studied the battle plans of samurai warriors who went before them.

Jack has shown again and again that his mind and spirit are just as strong as his body. His sharp mind has helped him trick his enemies when the odds were against him. And his strong spirit has kept him going when his body was out of energy. Without a discipline of mind, body, and spirit, Jack would have lost to Aku long ago.

Never Give Up

Once, Jack was about to reach a time portal, but an army of robot beetles destroyed it just before he reached it. Exhausted and disappointed, Jack decided to give up his quest. Then Jack met up with three monks who were going to climb an impossibly high mountain. According to legend, those who climbed the mountain would find Truth at the top. Jack joined the monks, hoping to find a way home. After facing many dangers, Jack made it to the top. He didn't find a time portal there, but he did learn that he could overcome any obstacle to reach his goal. Jack never gave up again.

THE WARRIOR SPIRIT

"*Nothing worth having is easily attained. Sometimes you must fight for what is yours — and what you believe in. It is not one's outward brawn, but rather one's inner strength, that makes them mighty.*"

Jack's father said these words to his son when Jack was just a young boy, and the samurai has never forgotten them. They describe what the warrior spirit is all about.

"*Nothing worth having is easily attained.*"

Trying to find a way back in time is definitely not easy. Jack has traveled the earth, following leads, only to find his hopes dashed again and again. But he doesn't give up, because a world without Aku is something worth having. His warrior spirit keeps him going.

"*Sometimes you must fight for what is yours — and what you believe in.*"

Every time Jack faces off against a robot army, or defends himself against alien hunters, he's fighting for a reason. He's fighting for his family, whose lives were destroyed by Aku so long ago. And he's fighting for the world the way it should be: a peaceful, beautiful world, free from Aku's destruction. That's what separates Samurai Jack from any other warrior — he's fighting for what he believes in.

"It is not one's outward brawn, but rather one's inner strength, that makes them mighty."

Jack could be the strongest man in the universe, but if he did not have inner strength, he would be nothing. Jack's strong inner spirit has kept him going when another person would have lost faith. It's what allows him to perform amazing feats, like singlehandedly destroying a huge army of robot beetles. He's not a superhero, and he doesn't have special powers. It's his belief in himself that makes him strong.

Samurai Jack has a long road ahead of him. Finding a way back to the past and destroying Aku will not be easy. But there's one thing you can be sure of — Jack's warrior spirit will keep him going until the job gets done.

GLOSSARY

BUSHIDO: The "way of the warrior." The code of conduct for the samurai.

DAIMYO: A high-ranking samurai who owned land.

JUJITSU: An unarmed style of martial arts.

KEN-JUTSU: The "way of the sword." The ancient art of samurai sword fighting.

RONIN: A samurai without a master.

SAMURAI: A member of the warrior class of Japan.

SHOGUN: The leader of the national army of Japan.